Dough-Pea Gets Lost

One day while I was digging in my garden, I discovered a village of little flowerpots. In this village lived the Poddington Peas.

The Peas soon became my friends, and began to tell me stories of their adventures. In return I promised to keep the secret of where they lived.

This is one of the many stories they told me.

Up in Creepy Castle, Creep-Pea sat at the head of his huge table, waiting for his supper. What would his loyal servant Black-eyed Pea have cooked for him tonight? Creep-Pea licked his lips as he imagined a tasty bowl of soup, followed by his favourite rock cakes. 'And a lovely creamy custard tart to finish,' he said to himself.

But as usual Creep-Pea was wrong. Black-eyed Pea served him the only thing he knew how to cook. It was burnt toast again!

Creep-Pea pushed the burnt toast away and looked out of the window of Creepy Castle. He could see someone in the distance. A busy figure was hurrying beyond the Creepy Carrot Patch, carrying a basket.

It was Dough-Pea the baker, on his unusual bread round. It was unusual because he always did it in the evening instead of the morning. But that's because he was Dough-Pea!

Creep-Pea rubbed his empty stomach and thought of warm, new bread. Then, as he watched Dough-Pea, he had an idea. If his plan worked, Creep-Pea's problems with meals would be over.

Next evening, as it was getting dark, Creep-Pea sneaked down from Creepy Castle to the signpost at the edge of the Creepy Carrot Patch. As the Carrots looked on, Creep-Pea switched the sign around.

Later that evening, Dough-Pea arrived at the signpost. 'That's strange,' he thought, 'this doesn't look like the way to Poddington. But who would be silly enough to switch the signpost around?'

Dough-Pea set off, following the sign for Poddington. He was looking forward to getting back to his bakery and having a leftover roll.

He didn't notice that he was walking right through the Creepy Carrot Patch. He didn't even notice that he was walking up through the Rockery and that Creepy Castle was looming above him.

The Creepy Carrots watched as Dough-Pea went right up to the door of Creepy Castle. They didn't want to cry out and warn him in case they ended up in one of his carrot cakes.

Dough-Pea looked at the sign hanging on the castle door. It said 'Bakery. (honest).' It didn't look at all like Dough-Pea's bakery. 'But if the sign says it is, I suppose it must be,' thought Dough-Pea. 'I expect I'd better knock.'

The door creaked open and Dough-Pea walked nervously inside. As the door slammed shut behind him, Creep-Pea

snarled, 'A-ha, a trespasser! Your punishment will be to spend the rest of your life cooking for me.'

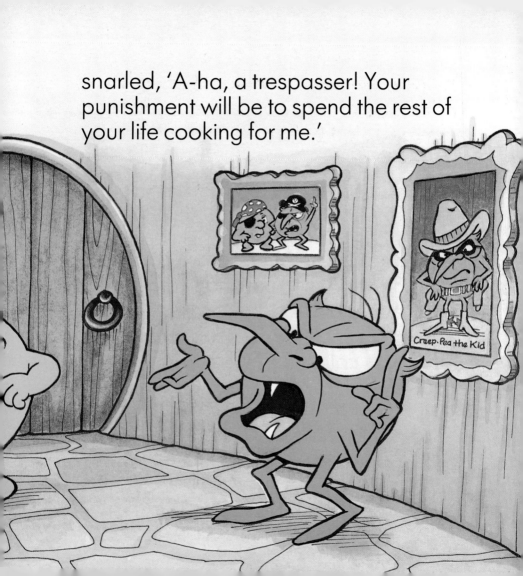

Dough-Pea was bundled down to the kitchen. 'We want our supper within the hour', warned Creep-Pea and Black-eyed Pea.

The kitchen was in a dreadful mess. The washing-up had not been done for at least a month, and there were cobwebs and dirt everywhere. Dough-Pea thought with longing of his clean, tidy bakery. He blew the dust off a large cook book which was called 'How To Burn Toast' by Black-eyed Pea.

There was no escape. Dough-Pea would have to cook Creep-Pea and Black-eyed Peas' supper. So he worked hard making cakes, a pot of soup and some custard. At last he was finished, and ready to present a three-course meal to his captors who were waiting impatiently upstairs.

Dough-Pea served the first course – a lovely nettle soup. Creep-Pea looked at the soup and stirred it.

'Hmm, this looks very tasty,' he said as he helped himself to an extra large spoonful.

But as soon as Creep-Pea had swallowed, he realised that the soup was made from raw nettles. His tongue was covered in nettle stings.

Creep-Pea was speechless as Dough-Pea brought on the second course – rock cakes. Creep-Pea loved these, and he bit into one hungrily, hoping to get rid of the taste of the horrible soup. But the rock cakes were made from real rocks and Creep-Pea's teeth shattered into pieces. He mumbled to Dough-Pea that the pudding had better be good, or there would be trouble.

The pudding was Creep-Pea's favourite – a lovely custard tart.

'Now this looks more like it,' he said, helping himself to a large slice.

He examined it carefully before taking a few nibbles from the end. But that was enough to send him flying from his chair, flames shooting out of his mouth. The tart was red hot. Instead of custard, Dough-Pea had used mustard!

Dough-Pea smiled nervously as he asked, 'Was the meal all right, Sir?'

That was the last straw. Creep-Pea and Black-eyed Pea marched Dough-Pea over the gangway of Creepy Castle and told him never to return. To make quite sure that he never did, Creep-Pea switched the signpost back again.

Back at his bakery, Dough-Pea was soon busy baking batches of bread and cakes. He never did go back to Creepy Castle, but he did send Creep-Pea a large, tasty loaf. Of course Black-eyed Pea made burnt toast with it, but funnily enough Creep-Pea thought it was just delicious.